Mr Croc was very busy.
It was Monday and he was doing
his washing.

He placed the washing on the kitchen table and looked out of the window. The bushes were swaying in the wind. 'It's very blowy today,' he said.

He filled the sink with hot water...

...put in his washing...

...and added some soap flakes.

He sloshed the water around to make it soapy... but nothing happened.

'That's odd,' said Mr Croc. 'Where are all the bubbles?' He looked at the packet and groaned. 'No wonder there are no bubbles,' he said.

Mr Croc was very forgetful.

He rinsed the porridge off his clothes and washed them again with soap flakes.

Then he put them through the mangle...

...and took them out into the windy garden.

'Washing day is turning out to be harder than usual,' said Mr Croc.

Mr Croc hung his washing on the line and watched as it flapped in the breeze.

He was just about to go back inside when he noticed something very strange.

The washing was flapping right off the line.

'Oh no!' yelped Mr Croc.

I forgot to use any clothes pegs!

Mr Croc ran round the garden chasing after his clothes.

After much puffing and panting, he managed to catch them all.

But as he pegged them back on to the line he noticed that something was missing.

There's only one sock!

Mr Croc searched all over the garden,
but he couldn't find the missing sock.
'It must have blown away,' he said.

Glumly he went back into the kitchen.
'I need cheering up,' he said.

I know! I'll make myself a triple-decker sardine sandwich!

Mr Croc liked fish.
But when he looked in the cupboard it was empty.

Oh no!
I forgot to buy any sardines!

I'll just have to go to the shops again.

Mr Croc put on his jacket and tied his
scarf. Then he smiled at himself in the
hall mirror.

'What a lovely smile I've got,' he
thought.

It cheered him up.

Mr Croc set off for the shops. He smiled his lovely smile at everyone he met.

At the shops he met his friend, Mr Hound.
'Hello, Mr Croc,' said Mr Hound.

Mr Croc stopped and scratched his head.

Mr Croc thought hard.

'I think... maybe... it had something to do with socks,' he said.

'Socks?' said Mr Hound. 'Funny you should say that.'

16

Mr Croc looked up.

'It's my sock!' replied Mr Croc.

Mr Croc reached up to get it...

...but as he did he caught sight of his reflection in the shop window.

He stopped and smiled his lovely smile.

What a lovely smile I've got.

Just then a gust of wind blew the sock
on to the arm of Mr Gloss, the painter.

As he shook it off,
Mr Gloss dropped
his paint pot.

But Mr Hound
caught it just
in time.

'I'm very sorry, Mr Gloss,' said Mr Croc.
'It's not really a snake...'

The sock sailed off down the street...

...flipping and
flapping in
the wind.

Mr Croc and Mr Hound ran after it...
puffing and panting in the wind.

21

They caught up with the sock at the
corner of the street.

It was
dangling
from a
lamp post.

Mr Croc streched up to get it...

...but as he did so, he saw himself
in the side mirror of a parked van.

Mr Croc smiled a lovely smile.

While Mr Croc was busy admiring himself, the sock flapped off the lamp post...

...and landed on Mrs Poodle's nose.
She yelped in suprise.

She stumbled across the pavement,
heading straight for the lamp post.

Mr Hound stopped her just in time.

'Sorry, Mrs Poodle,' said Mr Croc.

It's my sock.

It's a very silly sock!

Mrs Poodle hung the sock on the van's mirror and strode off.

As Mr Croc reached for the sock...

...BRRRM! The van drove off.

Mr Croc and Mr Hound chased after it.

The van stopped at the traffic lights.

But before Mr Croc could grab the sock, it
blew away once more...

...knocking Miss Siam's shopping list out
of her hands.

The list fluttered in the wind...

...but Mr Hound
leapt up and
caught it.

'Sorry, Miss Siam,' said Mr Croc.

'Oh dear,' said Mr Croc as Miss Siam walked off. 'My silly sock has caused such a lot of fuss. I'd better take it straight home.'

On his way home Mr Croc began to wonder what it was he had meant to buy at the shops.

But he couldn't remember.

Outside the park he saw Mr Gloss the painter, looking glum. 'What's wrong, Mr Gloss?' asked Mr Croc.

The wind blew my hat into that holly bush.

And I pricked my fingers trying to rescue it.

Mr Croc smiled his lovely smile.
'Allow me,' he said. He put the sock
over his hand...

...reached into
the holly bush,
and pulled out
Mr Gloss's hat.

Mr Gloss grinned.
'Smart thinking, Mr Croc,' he said.

Thank
you!

As Mr Croc set off again he
was still wondering
about what he
had meant
to buy.

Outside the hairdresser's he saw Mrs
Poodle. She was standing in the doorway
looking worried.

'What's wrong, Mrs Poodle?' asked
Mr Croc.
'I've just had a new hair-do,' she replied.

Mr Croc smiled his lovely smile.

Carefully
he placed
his sock
over her hair.

The sock made a very good hat and
Mrs Poodle reached her house with her
new hair-do still in place.

'Smart thinking, Mr Croc,' she said.

Thank
you!

Mr Croc set off again...
<u>still</u> wondering
about what he
had meant to buy.

On the corner he met Miss Siam.
She was looking sadly at her shopping
which was lying on the pavement.

'What's wrong, Miss Siam?' asked Mr Croc. Miss Siam sighed. 'My carrier bag burst,' she said.

Mr Croc smiled his lovely smile...

...and handed
Miss Siam
his sock.

'Why don't you borrow this?' he said.
'I've got big feet... so my sock will make
a roomy shopping bag!'

Miss Siam put all her
shopping in
Mr Croc's sock.

'Smart thinking, Mr Croc,' she said.

By now Mr Croc was nearly home.
But he was STILL
wondering about what
he had meant to buy.

Just then a bus went past.
It was full of shoppers.

Everyone is packed in like sardines in a tin!

Mr Croc gasped.

'Yes!' he cried. 'That's it!'

He rushed back to the shops...

...but he was too late.
All the shops were shut.

His tummy rumbled.

Mr Croc trudged home feeling very gloomy. But when he got there he found a surprise waiting for him.

Hanging on his door knob was his sock...

...and inside there were six tins of
sardines.

There was also a note inside the sock.

Dear Mr Croc,
    On my way home I met Mr Gloss and Mrs Poodle. They told me how you had helped them too. We all know how much you like fish so here are some sardines... just to say thank you.
        Enjoy them!
        Yours sincerely,
            Miss Siam

'Presents in my sock!' cried Mr Croc.
'Wonderful!'

He took the sock into the kitchen.
'Time for food!' he said. But as he
unpacked the sardines something
caught his eye.

Mr Croc rushed outside and gathered all the clothes from the line.

Then he ironed them...

...and put everything away...

...except his silly sock.

As he opened the tins, Mr Croc smiled his lovely smile. 'All's well that ends well,' he said.

The End